The Song of Her Soul

a short story

Wendi S. Harrington

White Fields Press LLC

The Song of Her Soul

©2025 Wendi S. Harrington

ISBN: 978-1-964351-45-2 paperback

ISBN: 997-9-8233959-60-8 eBook

Published by White Fields Press LLC
An Independent Apostolic Publishing Company
4019 W. Highway 70 PMB# 227
Durant OK 74701-4591
803-70-WRITE
(803-709-7483)
info@whitefieldspress.com
https://WhiteFieldsPress.com

White Fields
PRESS
An Independent Apostolic Publishing Company

Contents

The Song of Her Soul

a short story

Chloe's mom glanced at her curiously. Chloe tapped the home button and laid her phone on the table face-down. Her skin felt electrified as she finished her meal. She paid special attention to each bite as she chewed, careful not to choke. Surely she had read the message from Sis. Ava wrong. The urge to pick up her phone and reread it tempted her, but what if she'd understood it correctly?

Her mom glanced at her again.

Chloe took a slow drink of tea. Her palms and wrists itched. She rubbed her hands against her denim skirt.

Jack, her older brother, sat across the table, oblivious to her turmoil as he shoveled mac and cheese into his mouth with one hand while tapping the game on his phone with the other. He never even glanced her way.

Traitor.

Had he said something to Sis. Ava? He must have. How else would she know Chloe sang? She considered kicking him under the table, but she knew Mom would notice. Instead, she cleared her throat. "Could you take me to practice the parallel parking again after dinner?"

"Sure," he replied without taking his eyes off his phone.

"Thanks." Chloe pushed the food around her plate. Her stomach felt queasy. "Excuse me." She gave her mom a soft smile as she stood.

"You've barely eaten enough to feed a bird."

"I'm full. I ate a snack earlier."

Jack stood abruptly, slipping his phone into his back pocket. "Hold up. I'm ready." He picked his plate up and raked the rest of his food into his mouth. With bulging cheeks, he motioned toward the front door.

Chloe discarded her leftovers into the dog bowl and rinsed both their plates.

A block away from the house, Chloe slapped the dash, turning toward her brother. "What did you say to Sis. Ava?"

"Nothing. Why?"

"Because!" Chloe felt the burn along the side of her neck and left ear as she wrestled her phone from her skirt pocket. She tapped the message and turned it toward him. "She sent this."

"What does it say?"

Gritting her teeth, she read the message to him. "Hey, Chloe, I was wondering if you would sing a solo at the youth rally this month? Just let me know."

"Really?" He flashed his trademark smile at her. "That's great. I think you should do it."

"I. Don't. Sing." The sound of his laughter infuriated her. "What's so funny?"

"You sing all the time."

"Not for people!"

C hloe sat alone in her room and stared at her phone. She tried not to think about the third-grade talent show, but the memory forced its way into her mind. She could still hear Brian Daniels's mocking laughter as he repeated her blundered line ad nauseam.

She shook her head, frustrated.

Brian Daniels wouldn't be at the youth rally. He didn't go to any of the churches that hosted it.

But Janie Adams did. And she had been just as relentless as Brian in her daily attempts to humiliate Chloe. Marie Sanders would be there too. Even though Marie hadn't mocked Chloe after the show, she had been quick to laugh with those who did.

Chloe turned to the keyboard rigidly. Sis. Ava's response had been quick when Chloe declined the invitation.

> Will you pray about it before you decide? I felt heavily impressed to ask you.

Why would God want her to do this? Didn't he know how much she had been hurt? He *had* to know that's why she stopped talking at school. And she never did another talent show. Ever.

She tapped a single key, lost in thought, remembering the agonizing months she spent worrying that God would ignore her prayers if she didn't speak them out loud. Night after night, she had hidden in her room and tried to muster the courage to speak her prayers aloud.

Chloe began to play the keyboard and hum along.

It had been so hard to set her voice free, even here, in the privacy of her own room.

"Even if my voice is shaking." And it *was* shaking. But the sweet calm that came when she played was worth it. "Still, I know your love's unchanging." Moisture collected behind her eyes. Love swelled within her. She continued to sing. "In secret places, you would meet me. You held me when the tears would fall. You taught my heart to rise in worship. Though no one heard me sing at all."

That's the way she liked it. Her praise and worship were special, just between her and God. She didn't want to sing for other people. "Now I stand because you stayed. You healed the fear that once en-slaved. Jesus, I simply sing for you alone. This is the song, this is the song of my soul."

Jack clapped enthusiastically from the doorway, startling her. She twirled on her stool and clasped her hands in her lap.

"Wow. That's even better than the last one."

She felt her cheeks flame hotly. "How long have you been there?"

"Long enough to know that's a hit. Are you going to sing it at the rally?"

She shook her head. "No way. I'm not singing at the rally."

Jack's brow creased. "Why? You're so good."

"I don't want to."

"What if God called you to it?"

Her throat tightened. "He wouldn't do that."

Jack crossed his arms. "What about the talents? Remember the parable? God doesn't like it when we hide our talents. You have a beautiful voice. God gave you that for a reason."

The tears welled up. "Why would he ask me to do something he knows I can't do?"

Jack shrugged. "Maybe it's like that servant. The one who was afraid when they were surrounded, because he couldn't see God's army standing with them for the battle. Maybe you just can't see what God will do with your talent. Maybe you're just supposed to trust him."

When she didn't respond, he called her by her childhood nickname. "It's a good song, Coco. Pray about."

Pray about it.

Everyone kept saying that.

She DIDN'T talk to people. Why would she sing to them?

Pray about it.

Disappointment weighed heavily on Chloe's mind as she got dressed and went downstairs. After praying about the youth rally well into the night, she expected to wake up with a distinct answer. Yet, nothing had changed. She still didn't want to do it. She asked God why he would want her to do something that terrified her so much, and he had not responded.

"Quit scratching." Chloe's mom gripped her wrist and pulled it away from her neck. Leaning in, she examined the skin. "I don't see a bite or rash." She turned Chloe's hand over and surveyed the forearm. "Hives?" Her eyes settled on Chloe's. "What's wrong?"

Tears pricked the back of her eyes. Chloe blinked and shrugged. "Sis. Ava asked me to sing at the rally."

Her mom cupped a hand under Chloe's chin. "God gave you a beautiful voice." She leaned down and kissed Chloe's forehead. She held Chloe's gaze with her own and gently said, "It is the world that robbed you of your confidence. Don't be too quick to decline, Chloe." She smiled and stepped away. When she returned, she had coconut oil in her hand. "File your nails down some more. You've almost drawn blood." She rubbed coconut oil into Chloe's neck, hands, and forearms.

"Thanks, Mom." Chloe pushed the words around the lump in her throat. She wanted to say more, but couldn't.

"You're welcome." Her mom's voice faded as she stepped out of the room. She came back with a small book in her hand. "Look, I want to show you something."

Chloe leaned toward her to get a better look. It was a small devotional for busy moms. Her mother opened it near the middle and turned it around, pointing at the top of the page. Chloe read today's date at the top. "Okay."

Her mom tapped the passage below the date. "Read it."

Chloe pulled the book a little closer. "I will praise thee for ever, because thou hast done it: and I will wait on thy name; for it is good before thy saints. Psalm fifty-two and nine." Chloe bit her lip.

"Well?"

"Nice." She had to concentrate to keep from scratching in front of her mom. The itch along her neck and forearms had gained intensity.

"That's not a coincidence. Here. Keep it with you." She pushed the book toward Chloe.

"I'm not a busy mom."

"Nope, but you are a child of the King." Her mom picked up her coffee cup and disappeared into the kitchen.

Chloe carried the small book to her room.

C hloe knelt at the foot of her bed to pray again. She looked up all the verses in the Bible about weakness after class let out. She read about the sufficiency of God's grace and how perfect his strength was in weakness. Nothing allayed her fear; but every time she picked up her phone to text Sis. Ava and explain that she couldn't sing a solo; she felt an overwhelming disappointment in herself as though she had failed at something. She reread the verse in her mom's devotional and the passage below it that encouraged readers to praise God because of what he had already done and not because of man's ability.

Maybe singing at the rally wasn't about her voice or the performance at all.

She fell asleep thinking about the prophet's servant, frightened and exclaiming that the enemy had them surrounded until the prophet prayed and asked God to open the servant's eyes. Revealing the Lord's army.

C hloe woke up early on Saturday morning. She read her mom's devotional and prayed. As she dressed, she caught herself humming and made her way over to the keyboard. Tapping keys lightly, searching for the right chord, she found herself expanding the song she had worked on last week.

"I used to hide behind the silence, letting others make a joyful noise. My heart so longed to sing your praises — but I let fear drown out my voice. In secret places, you would meet me." Chloe continued to play and sing. Her heart soared with each new word that flowed. A tear slid down one cheek as she repeated the line she was working on. "This is the song... this is the song of my soul." She sang the line again before switching the keyboard off.

Jack's presence in the doorway startled her as she turned. His eyes glistened and his voice caught when he spoke. "Did you—" he cleared his throat. "Did you decide to do it?"

Chloe nodded.

"Are you going to sing that song?"

She glanced back at the keyboard and shook her head. "No. Just *Amazing Grace*, I think."

"But Chloe, that song is perfect."

She shrugged. "It's not finished."

"I can help you finish it." He stepped into her room, rubbing his palms together. "I can play and let you just focus on singing."

"I don't have time." She sank onto the foot of her bed. "And, besides, it's hard enough to sing without..." Her voice trailed off, and she scratched at her wrist.

Jack knelt in front of her. "You wouldn't have to worry about mixing up the words if you wrote them."

Fury shot through her spine. "Jack!" She shoved him hard enough to knock him off his feet.

"Hey!" He held both hands up in surrender. "I'm serious. I wasn't making fun."

"Well, it isn't funny!" She tightened her hands into fists as the memory of Brian Daniels's relentless mockery took shape in the forefront of her mind.

"I didn't say it was. I just mean, you wouldn't have to worry about it." He rose to his feet and took one of her hands in both of his. "Chloe, it's about worship, not performance."

His words cut through the memory of Brian Daniels's laughter. "What did you say?" She met his gaze with a bewildered stare.

Jack leaned down. "I said it's about worship. Not performance. And that song you just sang was pure worship."

She felt the smile forge its way across her face, even as the apprehension rose into her chest. "Do you really think so?"

"Yeah." He raked his fingers through his hair and shrugged, grinning back at her. "It's way better than the one you wrote a few months ago."

Her mind whirled. "It's just for Jesus."

"You can tell. That's what makes it so perfect."

"You'll really help me? Will you play at the rally, too?"

"Sure." He laughed. "I would be honored."

She squealed. "Am I crazy? Can I really do this?" She crossed her hands over her heart.

He tousled her hair. "Yes, you are. And yes, you can."

"I'm terrified."

"You'll do fine. I have faith in you."

She frowned. "I'm stuck on this one part. I can't quite get it right."

"Okay." He pulled her stool out and sat at the keyboard. "Let's work on it."

C hloe stood beside the platform door. Her nerves returned to taunt her. She tightened her grip on Jack's arm.

"You'll do fine," he whispered, leaning down.

"Did I tell you about my dream?" Was it okay to talk while someone else was singing? *Oh, Jesus, forgive me.*

Jack shook his head.

She rose on her tiptoes to whisper in his ear. "We went to the old mill to practice driving, and the whole parking lot was full of chariots."

"Chariots?"

She nodded and hurried on. "Made of some kind of special metal. Golden, but they seemed to glow and burn in the sunlight."

"Burn?"

"Yeah. It was like a gazillion candle flames. That's not important. Listen."

"Okay." Jack stifled a smile.

"The chariots drove past us. Each one held someone I knew. The first one was you, which was weird because you were in the car with me, but then you were in the chariot, too. And you said, 'That song is perfect, Coco.'"

"It is perfect."

"Listen!" Chloe smacked his arm and continued. "The next one was Mom, and she said something about God preparing me for this. Then Sis. Ava came by and thanked me for singing. And it just kept on. People from church. People from school. And you won't believe who else."

"Who?"

"Marie Sanders," Chloe grinned. "She came by and said this was an answered prayer."

"Wow," Jack smiled back.

"I know! It's just like that verse in Psalms."

"Which verse?"

"Fifty-two and nine. Mom showed it to me last week. It says, 'I will praise thee for ever, because thou hast done it.'"

The song on the platform ended. Chloe bowed her head and squeezed Jack's arm. She inhaled deeply and prayed. "This is for you, Lord. You've already done enough. In Jesus' name, Amen."

"Amen," Jack opened his eyes and looked at her as the announcer said her name and her church. "It's about worship, not about performance."

A wave of nausea and dizziness washed over her as they stepped out onto the platform. She felt her brother's arm steady her. "Just pure worship. It's not about them. It's about him."

"Right." She managed a weak smile. Her throat felt dry.

Jack handed her a microphone and stepped behind the keyboard. Why hadn't she just played the keyboard herself? Then she wouldn't have to stand here exposed. A sea of faces swam before her, and her nausea strengthened, weakening her resolve. The opening of the song came, but she missed it.

Jack continued to play.

The opening of the song came again, and Chloe met it with a trembling voice. "I used to hide behind the silence, letting others make a joyful noise. My heart so longed to sing your praises — but I let fear drown out my voice. In secret places, you would meet me. You held me when the tears would fall. You taught my heart to rise in worship, though no one heard me sing at all."

Chloe spotted Marie Sanders in the crowd. Her golden-brown eyes widened as Chloe's gaze met hers. Apprehension took a firm hold on Chloe's heart and squeezed. Marie lifted praying hands to her chin and smiled toward the ceiling. Was she crying? The fear and apprehension drifted away as Chloe watched Marie lift her hands in praise. Her lips trembled, and she made no effort to hide her tears.

Chloe closed her eyes and pictured Marie Sanders in the glowing chariot, candlelight flickering in her eyes as she said this was an answered prayer. By the time Chloe finished the second verse, she had forgotten the crowd was there. "You're still the one who sets me free."

Tears streamed down her face as she continued. She opened her eyes and fixed them on the cross between the doorways. "I won't let fear rewrite my story. I won't let silence steal your glory, even when my voice is shaking. The Bible says your love's unchanging. You gave me this song to sing so I could praise the King of Kings."

A calm confidence settled over her. This was what she was meant to do. Her purpose in the church. Her role in the body of Christ. Pure worship. It always had been. Her voice wasn't perfect. She might miss the words sometimes. But Chloe had stepped into the plans God had made for her, and she knew it with a certainty that could never again be shaken.

"This is the song of my soul. Your melody that made me whole. Even when the fear returns, your fire in me will continue to burn. I will sing through every tear. It's your love that brought me here. Jesus, you have made me whole. This is the song... This is the song... This is the song... This is the song of my soul."

It wasn't perfect. Chloe didn't care. It was heartfelt, and people all over the sanctuary were lifting their hands and their voices in worship. It wasn't about her. It had never been. It was about lifting him up and giving him honor. She looked around the room and knew God was being glorified.

As they left the platform, Jack wrapped an arm around her and pulled her against him. Planting a kiss on the top of her head, he simply said, "Proud of you, Coco."

The song she sang felt like ancient history by the time Chloe finished the after-service meal and headed for the dessert table. The preacher had taken a deep dive into the identity change that comes with following the Lord. From Abraham to Paul, he contrasted who they were before with who they became after an encounter with the Lord. Chloe had to stop writing once and shake out her hand as she took notes. He spent more time on Jacob, lingering on the way Jacob wrestled with the angel and walked away from that encounter blessed but marked by a permanent limp.

She wondered if her silence over the years had equated to wrestling with God — throwing away her birthright, like Esau. Truly praising God and fulfilling the great commission required more than hiding in a bedroom with secret praises. How could she tell others about the Lord Jesus Christ if she didn't even speak to them? She had made her way to the altar as soon as the service ended and prayed for forgiveness of her selfishness and fear. She offered her voice to the Lord, in song or in speech, no matter the situation or audience.

The peace that settled around her at the altar was still holding her now as she perused the cakes and pies in search of the perfect slice.

"I've been praying for you."

Chloe knew who the soft voice belonged to before she turned to look into Marie's golden-brown eyes. Chloe could almost see the flicker of candlelight reflected there.

"For a few years now." Marie blinked back a tear. Her lip trembled. "We were just dumb kids. I never meant to hurt you. Please forgive me."

Chloe offered a genuine smile. "I have. And thank you. Your prayers helped."

Marie smiled back. "I've always loved your voice. I thought I would never get to hear you sing again. Tonight was an answer to my prayers in so many ways." She switched her purse to the other shoulder and linked arms with Chloe. "God is so good! Let's celebrate. What kind of cake are you getting?"

Chloe pointed to a turtle cheesecake.

Marie scooped up two servings. "Can I join you?"

"Sure."

C hloe sat cross-legged on her bed with her journal in her lap. She drew the words in large, curling-vine letters with blossoms scattered around them, filling the whole page.

—Psalm 52:9 —-

I will praise thee for ever, because thou hast done it.

And he most certainly had. Three weeks had passed, and it still amazed her the way a prayer from one person wove perfectly into another prayer from someone else until God did just one thing, and every-one's prayers were answered together. Only God could do that. Ava had been praying for more youth involved in the choir. Jack had been praying for more time to practice the keyboard. Her mom had been praying that Chloe would regain her confidence and her voice. Her dad had been praying Chloe would make more friends. And Marie had been praying for forgiveness.

Those were just the prayers Chloe knew about.

Who could bring that all together into a single song?

Only God.

Chloe hummed a new melody as she finished drawing the decorative verse across the page.

And I will wait on thy name; for it is good before thy saints.

The End

This short story was written in response to Weekend Writing Prompt #141.
Come write with me!
Visit WeekendWritingPrompts.com to sign up.

The Song of My Soul

I used to hide behind the silence, letting others make a joyful noise. My heart so longed to sing your praises — but I let fear drown out my voice. In secret places, you would meet me. You held me when the tears would fall. You taught my heart to rise in worship, though no one heard me sing at all.

Now I stand because you stayed. You healed the fear that once enslaved. Jesus, I simply sing for you alone. This is the song, this is the song of my soul.

Even if my voice is shaking. Still, I know your love's unchanging. You're still the one who sets me free

I won't let fear rewrite my story. I won't let silence steal your glory, even when my voice is shaking. The Bible says your love's unchanging. You gave me this song to sing so I could praise the King of Kings.

This is the song of my soul. Your melody that made me whole. Even when the fear returns, your fire in me will continue to burn. I will sing through every tear. It's your love that brought me here. Jesus, you have made me whole. This is the song... This is the song... This is the song... This is the song of my soul.

Scan the QR code
to hear Chloe's song
on YouTube

Companion Devotional

The Song of Her Soul

Focus Scripture

"I will praise thee for ever, because thou hast done it: and I will wait on thy name; for it is good before thy saints."
Psalm 52:9 (KJV)

Reflect

Have you ever been asked to do something you were scared to try? Something that made your stomach twist and your heart pound? Chloe felt that way when Sis. Ava asked her to sing at the youth rally. But it wasn't just about fear—it was about remembering why we worship in the first place.

When we focus on performance, we worry about what others think. But when we focus on worship, we remember what God has already done. That's what Psalm 52:9 reminds us: we praise not for attention, but for God's past faithfulness.

Lesson

- - "Because Thou Hast Done It" — God has already proven Himself faithful.

- - "I Will Wait on Thy Name" — Waiting on God means trusting His timing.

- - "For It Is Good Before Thy Saints" — Your worship encourages others.

Personal Challenge

Is there something God is nudging you to do? Like Chloe, maybe your story is more about obedience than perfection.

Prayer Prompt

Jesus, thank You for what You've already done. Help me stop focusing on what I can't do and start trusting in what You've already done. I want to worship You with my whole heart—even when my voice is trembling. Amen.

Journal Prompt

1. Write about something God has already done in your life that you can praise Him for today:

2. Write one thing you're scared to do but feel God might be asking of you:

THE SONG OF HER SOUL

Activity Pages

The Song of Her Soul

Verse Mapping

Break down Psalm 52:9 into parts. What does each part mean in your own words? Use arrows or drawings.

Song Lyrics Brainstorm

Like Chloe, write a chorus or verse from your heart to God. Start with: "I will praise You because..."

Worship Over Worry Chart

Draw two columns. On the left, list the things you worry about. On the right, write how worship reminds you of God's power in each one.

Bible Tie-In

Read 2 Corinthians 12:9 and Isaiah 40:31. How do these verses connect with Psalm 52:9 and Chloe's story? Write or draw your thoughts.

Group Discussion Starters

- What does 'pure worship' mean to you?

- Have you ever let fear silence you?

- Why is praising God for what He's already done powerful?

About the Author

Wendi S. Harrington is an Apostolic author, nurse, and storyteller from southeastern Oklahoma with a heart for souls and a pen full of purpose. She writes Christian fiction, poetry, and devotionals that reflect the beauty of Apostolic faith and the hope found in Jesus. Rooted in truth, Wendi's stories are shaped by real-life sorrow and joy, and always written to stir the soul.

She is the author of *While Your Dreams Are Coming True* and additional short stories that speak to the heart of healing, redemption, and the power of prayer.

Want to stay connected? Visit **ApostolicFiction.com** to explore more of Wendi's writing and sign up for **Behind the Pages: Author Updates from Wendi S. Harrington**—a monthly peek into her life, inspiration, and upcoming releases.

Other Short Stories Available

As Long As It Takes
Hear My Prayer
The Mask She Wore
The Song of Her Soul
The Sound Of Silence

ApostolicFiction.com/ShortStories

www.ingramcontent.com/pod-product-compliance
Lightning Source LLC
Chambersburg PA
CBHW020321150626
46552CB00022B/3116